froglets

ANIMAL OLYMPICS

Ana Anteater
Goes for
Gold

Animal
Olympic Games

coming Soon

by Karen Wallace and Andy Rowland

W
FRANKLIN WATTS
LONDON•SYDNEY

Franklin Watts
First published in Great Britain in 2016
by the Watts Publishing Group

ISBN 978 1 4451 4770 3 (hbk)
ISBN 978 1 4451 4772 7 (pbk)
ISBN 978 1 4451 4771 0 (library ebook)

Series Editor: Melanie Palmer
Series Advisor: Catherine Glavina
Series Designer: Peter Scoulding

Printed in China

Franklin Watts
an imprint of Hachette Children's Group
Part of the Watts Publishing Group
Carmelite House
50 Victoria Embankment
London EC4Y 0DZ

An Hachette UK Company
www.hachette.co.uk

www.franklinwatts.co.uk

To Kit, Nico and Alec – K.W.

Ana Anteater loved
swimming with her friends.

They held hands and
swam in circles.

They leapt and they
twirled and they dived
in the water.

And they did everything
at exactly the same time.

"Amazing!" said Leopard
from his branch over
the pond.

"What kind of
swimming is that?"

"It's called synchronized
swimming," said Ana.

The next day, big news arrived in the jungle. A great competition was to be held in the city.

Animals from all over
the world were coming
to compete.

"We're going for a gold medal!" said Ana. So every day Ana and her friends swam from morning to night.

The trainers said they were fantastic but there was still something missing.

"Winners have magic," said the trainers. "What's special about Team Anteater?"

No one spoke. Then Ana thought of ants and the answer came to her.

The special thing about anteaters is their long, bendy tongues!

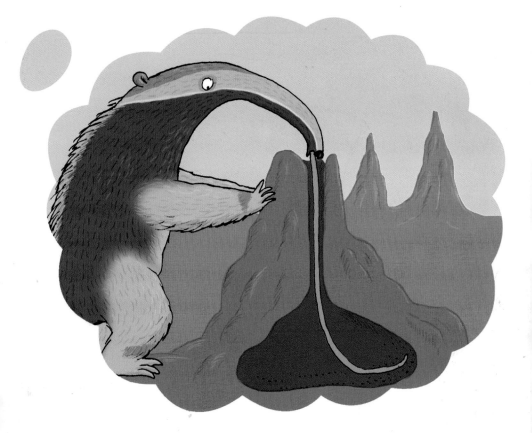

At last it was the day of
the competition.
"Team Anteater is next!"
said the judges.

TEAM
ANTEATER

A whistle blew and the
anteaters jumped into
the water.

They twirled and they twisted. They pointed their fingers.

Then they did something special. The anteaters locked toes and spun in a circle.

And they stuck out their tongues to make the shape of a star!

"Magic!" cried the judges. "Team Anteater wins the gold medal!"

Puzzle 1

Put these pictures in the correct order.
Now tell the story in your own words.
How short can you make the story?

happy bored

proud

scared pleased

relaxed

Choose the words which best describe the characters. Can you think of any more? Pretend to be one of the characters!

Answers

Puzzle 1

The correct order is:

1d, 2f, 3e, 4b, 5c, 6a

Puzzle 2

The correct words are happy, proud.

The incorrect word is bored.

The correct words are pleased, relaxed.

The incorrect word is scared.

Look out for more stories:

Robbie's Robot
ISBN 978 1 4451 3950 0 (HB)

The Green Machines
ISBN 978 1 4451 3954 8 (HB)

The Cowboy Kid
ISBN 978 1 4451 3946 3 (HB)

Dani's Dinosaur
ISBN 978 1 4451 3942 5 (HB)

Gerald's Busy Day
ISBN 978 1 4451 3934 0 (HB)

Billy and the Wizard
ISBN 978 0 7496 7985 9

The Frog Prince and the Kitten
ISBN 978 1 4451 1620 4

Bill's Scary Backpack
ISBN 978 0 7496 9468 5

Bill's Silly Hat
ISBN 978 1 4451 1617 4

Little Joe's Boat Race
ISBN 978 0 7496 9467 8

Little Joe's Horse Race
ISBN 978 1 4451 1619 8

Felix, Puss in Boots
ISBN 978 1 4451 1621 1

Cheeky Monkey's Big Race
ISBN 978 1 4451 1618 1

The Animals' Football Cup
ISBN 978 0 7496 9477 7

The Animals' Football Camp
ISBN 978 1 4451 1616 7

The Animals' Football Final
ISBN 978 1 4451 3879 4

That Noise!
ISBN 978 0 7496 9479 1

Cheeky Monkey's Big Race
ISBN 978 1 4451 1618 1

For details of all our titles go to: www.franklinwatts.co.uk